DIRT BIKE CRAZY

HUSQVARNA DIRT BIKES

By R. L. Van

Kaleidoscope
Minneapolis, MN

The Quest for Discovery Never Ends

This edition is co-published by agreement between
Kaleidoscope and World Book, Inc.

Kaleidoscope Publishing, Inc.
6012 Blue Circle Drive
Minnetonka, MN 55343 U.S.A.

World Book, Inc.
180 North LaSalle St., Suite 900
Chicago IL 60601 U.S.A.

Kaleidoscope ISBNs
978-1-64519-096-7 (library bound)
978-1-64494-152-2 (paperback)
978-1-64519-195-7 (ebook)

World Book ISBN
978-0-7166-4364-7 (library bound)

Library of Congress Control Number
2019939017

Printed in the United States of America.

Bigfoot lurks within one of the images in this book. It's up to you to find him!

TABLE OF CONTENTS

Chapter 1: Husky Race 4
Chapter 2: Husqvarna's Heritage 10
Chapter 3: The Huskies 16
Chapter 4: Husqvarna Stars 22

Beyond the Book 28
Research Ninja 29
Further Resources 30
Glossary 31
Index 32
Photo Credits 32
About the Author 32

CHAPTER 1

Husky Race

The **motocross** race is about to start. Zoey walks up to her Husqvarna TC 250. Lots of people call Husqvarna bikes Huskies. She likes that. It makes her think of the dog breed. The dogs race in snow. But her Husky races on dirt.

Zoey leans over. She pops out the **kick-starter**. Then she hops onto the blue seat. She pushes the kick-starter down with her foot. The bike roars to life. Many Husqvarna bikes have electric starts. But Zoey thinks the kick-starter is more fun.

Zoey places her feet on the pegs. They have spikes for her shoes to grip. Zoey adjusts her helmet. Then she grabs the handles. Her bike has Pro Taper handlebars. They handle the bumps in the track well. The metal is more flexible than on other handlebar brands.

The Husqvarna TC 250 is a good choice for motocross.

Motocross races take place on dirt tracks.

Zoey uses the **clutch** lever at her left hand. It helps her put the bike in **gear**. She rolls the **throttle** toward her. Zoom! She heads for the starting line. Zoey sees her parents and little brothers waving at her. She waves back. Then she turns back to her bike. She needs to focus.

The gate drops. The race begins. Zoey shoots forward! She didn't get the best start. Some other racers are ahead of her. But they're approaching a turn. Her bike turns easily. It is light and balanced. And it **accelerates** well out of a turn. Zoey passes more racers.

FUN FACT

Husqvarna also makes motorcycles for street use and pro racing.

PARTS OF A
HUSQVARNA TC 250

Zoey's bike is powerful. It has a two-stroke engine. Two-strokes are lighter and faster than four-strokes. They're also harder to control. Most of the racers have four-strokes. They're much easier to ride. But the Husqvarna TC 250 has great control. Zoey drives over hills and bumps. The bike doesn't bounce too much. She doesn't lose speed. Zoey has won against four-strokes before. She pulls ahead of the leader. She knows she can do it again.

Motocross riders power through hills and jumps to victory.

CHAPTER 2

Husqvarna's Heritage

In 1689, the king of Sweden made a command. He wanted to create a weapons factory. It would be in the city of Husqvarna. The Husqvarna company was founded. It made weapons for the king. Later, it made sewing machines and kitchen appliances. In 1903, Husqvarna started selling motorized bicycles.

Husqvarna has made dirt bikes since the 1950s.

The company improved its bikes over the years. Motocross became popular. Races were organized around Europe in the 1950s. Husqvarna built a motorcycle for off-road use. Husqvarna was off to the races!

FUN FACT

The first Husqvarna off-road bike was called the Silverpilen. This is Swedish for "silver arrow."

Rolf Tibblin climbed onto his red bike. He hadn't always been good at motorcycle racing. But he joined a motorcycle club in Sweden. He learned from friends. He practiced and improved. Tibblin started winning races. He rode a Husqvarna bike. He won the 250cc European motocross championship in 1959. And he won the 500cc world title in 1962. The next year, he was set to do it again.

Early Husqvarna bikes were red. Now they're blue and yellow.

It was the final race of the series. It was on a hilly track. An old castle stood nearby. Tibblin's Husqvarna was much lighter than the other bikes. He slid around a corner. The crowd watched him kick up sand. He crossed the finish line. A checkered flag waved. Tibblin had won the world title!

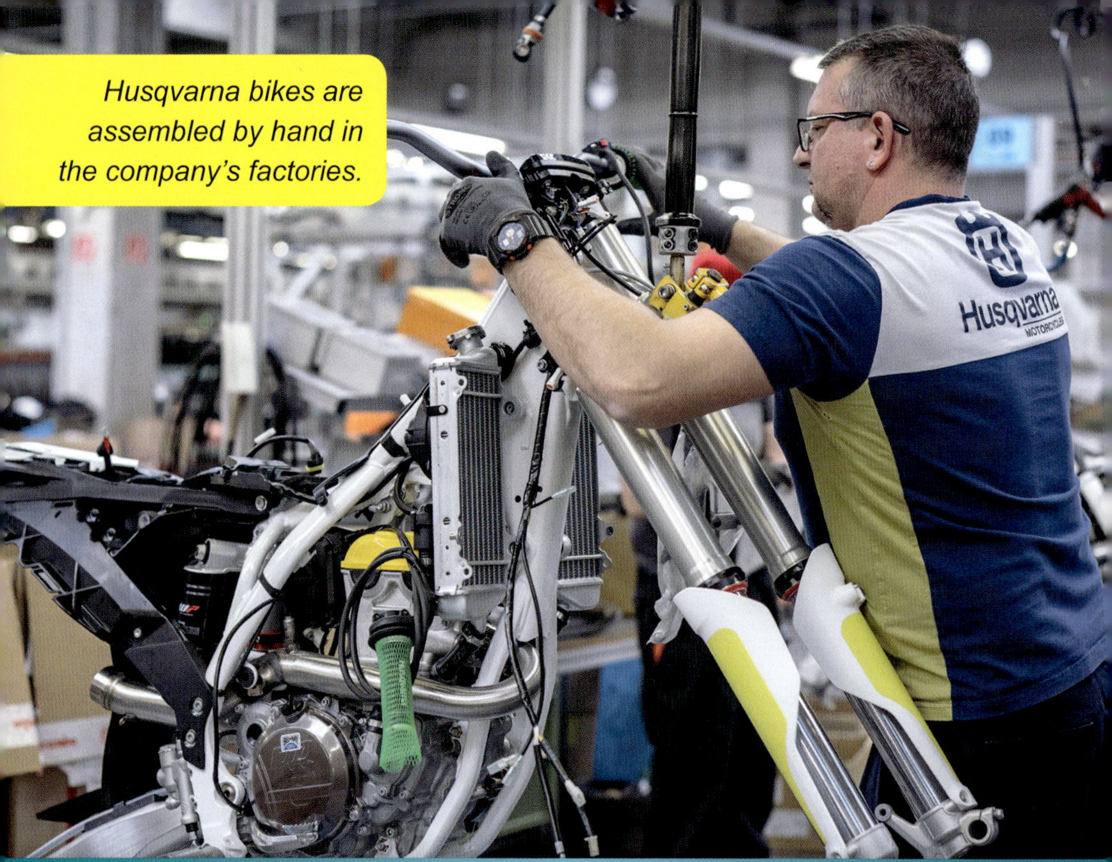

Husqvarna bikes are assembled by hand in the company's factories.

Husqvarna dominated the motocross scene. The 1960s and 1970s were Husky golden years. Husqvarna riders won fourteen world titles. They won enduros and rallies, too. These are off-road competitions.

In 1983, Husqvarna made a change. It took the red off its bikes. Now its bikes were all yellow, blue, and white. Its 500cc dirt bike had a new style. It was lightweight and easy to handle. Since then, Husqvarna has continued to improve. It had record sales in 2014. And it's kept up this winning streak. Husqvarna says it's been "Pioneering since 1903." The company lives up to its motto.

SWEDISH STYLE

Husqvarna dirt bikes are known for their colors. The colors are part of the company's Swedish heritage. Sweden's flag is blue and yellow. Husqvarna also tries to keep its Swedish values. It works toward traits like calmness and simplicity.

CHAPTER 3

The Huskies

Owen climbs onto his Husqvarna FC 350. It has a white front fender. Its yellow fork guards stand out. The navy blue seat is grippy. This keeps Owen on the bike.

Owen's bike is made for motocross racing. Only one other brand makes 350cc motocross bikes. This engine size is unusual. But Owen loves it. It's easy to turn like a 250. It's almost as powerful as a 450. But it feels lighter. This balance makes it easier to ride.

Owen races around the motocross track. He rides over bumps and hills. The bike absorbs shock well. This is thanks to its **air fork**. It also has good brakes. The bike stops easily when Owen needs it to.

The FC 350 is a motocross bike.

FUN FACT
Husqvarna is the world's oldest motorcycle maker with continuous production.

The FE 450 is good for riding on trails.

Owen's friend Trey is an enduro racer. He has a Husqvarna FE 450. It's a dual-sport bike. That means he can ride it on the track and off-road. Owen loves motocross. But he thinks enduro sounds fun. Sometimes, they go trail riding together. Trey lets Owen try out his FE 450. Trey rides his older brother's enduro bike.

The FE 450 looks like Owen's bike. They have some of the same features. Trey's bike has electric start, just like Owen's. And both bikes have air forks. But they don't drive the same. Trey's engine is more powerful. But it isn't as noisy as Owen's. The bike also has a headlight and turn signals. These help make it street legal. Trey can drive it on roads.

Owen and Trey drive up a mountain trail. Trey's bike travels over rocks and bumps easily. Its **suspension** absorbs the shock. The bike's foot pegs are higher than on a motocross bike. They don't get caught on obstacles. Owen's bike can power through mud and dirt on the motocross track. But it would be tough to drive here. Maybe Owen will get a cross-country bike like Trey's someday. For now, he wants to stick with his FC 350. He thinks it will make him a motocross champion.

BIKE MODEL	TC 250	FC 350	FE 450
SUITABLE FOR	Motocross	Motocross	Enduro/ Dual-Sport
ENGINE TYPE	Two-stroke	Four-stroke	Four-stroke
TYPE OF START	Kick-starter	Electric Starter	Electric Starter
WEIGHT	212 pounds (96 kg)	220 pounds (100 kg)	240 pounds (109 kg)
BASE PRICE	$8,299	$9,799	$11,099

HUSQVARNA DIRT BIKES

TC 250

FC 350

FE 450

CHAPTER 4

Husqvarna Stars

Husqvarna has many star athletes on its racing team. Their Huskies carry them to victory. One star is Jason Anderson. He races in supercross. He rides a Husqvarna FC 450.

Anderson raced in the Monster Energy AMA Supercross Championship. He was an underdog in 2018. People didn't expect him to win. But he stayed in the lead for much of the season. At the second-to-last round, Anderson had a shot. He wanted to get fifth or better. Then he'd secure the title early. But the pressure got to him. He came in seventeenth. He had to do better in the final round.

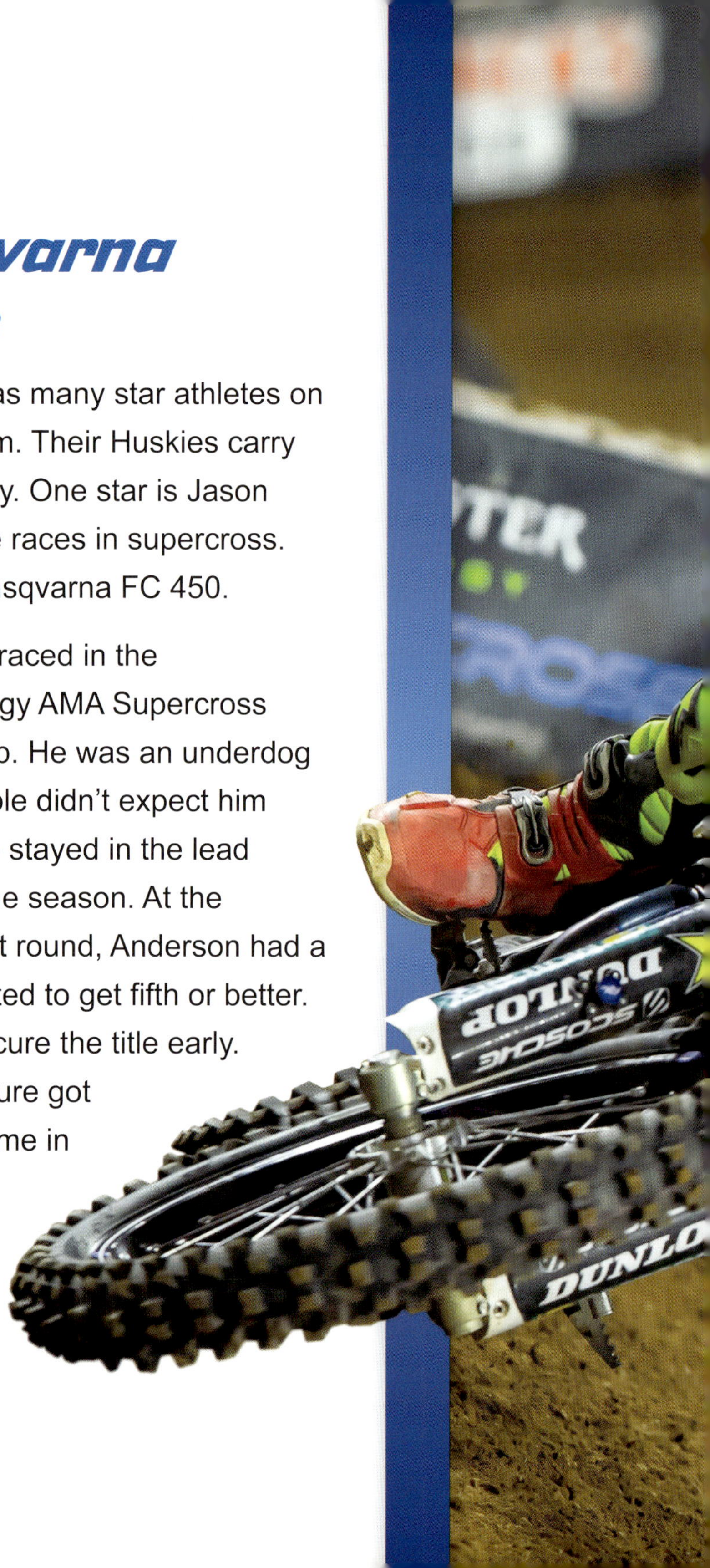

Jason Anderson races supercross inside stadiums.

Anderson rides an FC 450.

Anderson lined up at the championship race. The gate dropped. Anderson started out in sixth. He zipped over hills. The arena was crowded with tricky obstacles and sharp turns. He had to finish in the top ten. Anderson zoomed across the finish line. He got fifth place. That got him enough points. He won the series! It was his first supercross title. It was Husqvarna's first, too.

Chilean Pablo Quintanilla also competes for Husqvarna. He rides an FR 450. He races in rallies. Rallies are long races like enduros. Races can be thousands of miles long. Sometimes they last weeks! Rallies also test riders' navigation skills.

FUN FACT

Quintanilla was a thirteen-time motocross champion in Chile.

Quintanilla is a rally racer for Husqvarna.

Quintanilla drove through the thick desert sand. There was no path. It was the final day of the 2019 Dakar Rally in Peru. Quintanilla was in the lead overall for the series. He was giving it his all. He flew over a huge sand dune. But he landed hard on his foot. He fell off of his bike. A medical crew arrived to help him. He could have given up. But he climbed back on his bike. Quintanilla came in fourth place overall. He was happy he gave one hundred percent at the Dakar Rally.

Husqvarna has riders all over the world. They race as pros and as **amateurs**. They compete and ride for fun. No matter how they use their Huskies, they're proud to ride Husqvarna.

Quintanilla rides an FR 450.

BEYOND THE BOOK

After reading the book, it's time to think about what you learned. Try the following exercises to jumpstart your ideas.

THINK

THAT'S NEWS TO ME. The text mentions that Pablo Quintanilla competed in the 2019 Dakar Rally. How might news sources be able to fill in more detail about this? What new information could you find in news articles? Where could you go to find those sources?

CREATE

PRIMARY SOURCES. A primary source is an original document, photograph, or interview. Make a list of different primary sources you might be able to find about Husqvarna dirt bikes. What new information might you learn from these sources?

SHARE

SUM IT UP. Write one paragraph summarizing the important points from this book. Make sure it's in your own words. Don't just copy what is in the text. Share the paragraph with a classmate. Does your classmate have any comments about the summary? Do they have additional questions about Husqvarna dirt bikes?

GROW

REAL-LIFE RESEARCH. What places could you visit to learn more about Husqvarna dirt bikes? What other things could you learn while you were there?

RESEARCH NINJA

Visit *www.ninjaresearcher.com/0967* to learn how to take your research skills and book report writing to the next level!

RESEARCH

DIGITAL LITERACY TOOLS

SEARCH LIKE A PRO
Learn about how to use search engines to find useful websites.

FACT OR FAKE?
Discover how you can tell a trusted website from an untrustworthy resource.

TEXT DETECTIVE
Explore how to zero in on the information you need most.

SHOW YOUR WORK
Research responsibly—learn how to cite sources.

WRITE

GET TO THE POINT
Learn how to express your main ideas.

PLAN OF ATTACK
Learn prewriting exercises and create an outline.

DOWNLOADABLE REPORT FORMS

Further Resources

BOOKS

Abdo, Kenny. *Dirt Bikes*. Abdo Publishing, 2018.

Adamson, Thomas K. *Motocross Racing*. Bellwether Media, 2016.

Shaffer, Lindsay. *Dirt Bikes.* Bellwether Media, 2019.

WEBSITES

FACTSURFER

Factsurfer.com gives you a safe, fun way to find more information.

1. Go to www.factsurfer.com.
2. Enter "Husqvarna Dirt Bikes" into the search box and click 🔍.
3. Select your book cover to see a list of related websites.

Glossary

accelerates: If something accelerates, it goes faster. The bike accelerates from the starting line.

air fork: An air fork connects the bike's frame to its front wheel and provides suspension with air pressure. Owen's dirt bike easily handles bumps on the track thanks to its air fork.

amateurs: Amateurs are athletes who aren't paid to compete. There are separate competitions for amateurs and professionals.

clutch: The clutch is the part of the dirt bike that lets the rider change gears. Owen held down the clutch to put his bike in gear.

gear: A gear is a setting on a dirt bike that adjusts how the engine sends power to the wheels. Zoey shifted gears on her bike so she could ride up a hill.

kick-starter: A kick-starter is a lever on a dirt bike's engine that riders kick down in order to start the bike. Some riders prefer a kick-starter to an electric starter.

motocross: Motocross is a racing competition where riders drive dirt bikes around a dirt track. Zoey loves the excitement of motocross racing.

suspension: A vehicle's suspension keeps it steady over obstacles and absorbs shock. Husqvarna's off-road bikes have excellent suspension.

throttle: The throttle controls how much fuel or power can go to the engine. The throttle is on the right side of the handlebars.

Index

air forks, 8, 16, 19
Anderson, Jason, 22–24

colors, 4, 12, 14, 15, 16

Dakar Rally, 26
dual-sport bikes, 19, 20

enduro, 14, 19, 20, 25
engine size, 16

FC 350, 16, 20–21
FE 450, 19, 20–21

handlebars, 4

kick-starters, 4, 8, 20

motocross, 4–9, 11–13, 14, 16, 19, 20–21, 25

Quintanilla, Pablo, 25–26

rallies, 14, 25–26

Silverpilen, 11
street-legal bikes, 19
supercross, 22–24
suspension, 9, 16, 20
Sweden, 10, 12, 15

TC 250, 4–9, 20–21
Tibblin, Rolf, 12–13
two-stroke engines, 9, 20

PHOTO CREDITS

The images in this book are reproduced through the courtesy of: Dario Dominin/Shutterstock Images, front cover; Mitterbauer H./Husqvarna Motorcycles Media, pp. 3, 15 (bike); Sebas Romero/Husqvarna Motorcycles Media, p. 4; Schedl R./Husqvarna Motorcycles Media, pp. 5, 9, 19; Marco Campelli/Husqvarna Motorcycles Media, pp. 6–7, 14, 30; Husqvarna Motorcycles Media, pp. 8, 21 (top), 21 (middle), 21 (bottom); Kenneth Olausson/Husqvarna Motorcycles Media, pp. 10–11, 12–13; Herbert Kronfeld/ullstein bild/Getty Images, p. 12; Globe Turner/Shutterstock Images, p. 15 (flag); Sebas Romero/Husqvarna Motorcycles Media, pp. 16–17; Lackner F./Husqvarna Motorcycles Media, p. 18; Red Line Editorial, pp. 20–21; Simon Cudby/Husqvarna Motorcycles Media, pp. 22–23, 24, 24 (inset); Marcin Kin/Husqvarna Motorcycles Media, p. 25; Rally Zone/Husqvarna Motorcycles Media, p. 26–27, 27.

ABOUT THE AUTHOR

R. L. Van is a writer and editor from Minnesota. She loves books, animals, and crossword puzzles.